Prehistoric Creatures Then and Now

STEGOSAURUS

By K.S. Rodriguez

Illustrated by Patrick O'Brien

Steadwell Books

Raintree Steck-Vaughn Publishers

A Harcourt Company

Austin · New York

www.steck-vaughn.com

For dino-mite friends Mario and Sarah Artecona

Produced by By George Productions, Inc.

Published by Raintree Steck-Vaughn Publishers, an imprint of Steck-Vaughn Company

Library of Congress Cataloging-in-Publication Data
Rodriguez, K.S.
  Stegosaurus / by K.S. Rodriguez
      p.   cm — (Prehistoric creatures then and now)
  Summary: Describes the characteristics and habits of the plant-eating dinosaur, as well as theories about why it became extinct.
Includes index.
    ISBN 0-7398-0102-3
    Stegosaurus — Juvenile literature. [1. Stegosaurus.
2 Dinosaurs.]   I. Title. II. Series.
  QE862.O65 R65   2000
  567.915'3 — dc21   99-055478

Printed and bound in the United States of America
10 9 8 7 6 5 4 3 2 1 LB 02 01 00

Photo Acknowledgments:
Page 21: Department of Library Services, American Museum of Natural History; Page 23: Royal Tyrrell Museum of Paleontology/Alberta Community Development; Page 29: Museum of the Rockies, photo by Bruce Seylem.

Contents

The Age of Dinosaurs

It is a warm summer day. In a swampy meadow, a huge reptile is grazing on low plants. It is 9 to 11 feet (2.7 to 3.3 m) tall and 20 to 30 feet (6 to 9 m) long—the size of a large truck. Strange, leaf-shaped plates grow out of its back. Sharp spikes stick out of its tail.

Suddenly the animal is surprised by a fierce, meat-eating Allosaurus. The heavy creature is a dinosaur, too. It cannot run fast. Its only hope is to defend itself with its tail spikes.

This odd reptile may be hard to imagine. After all it is not alive today. It is the dinosaur Stegosaurus.

Stegosaurus may have lived in groups.

Dinosaur means "terrible large lizard." Dinosaurs lived on land about 245 million to 65 million years ago—long, long before the first human being was ever born.

Time Line ───────

Mesozoic
(The era of the dinosaurs)

prosauropod

Stegosaurus

Tyrannosaurus rex

Triassic	**Jurassic**	**Cretaceous**
245 million to 208 million years ago	208 million to 145 million years ago	145 million to 65 million years ago

 6

All dinosaurs were reptiles. All dinosaurs laid eggs. But not all dinosaurs were fearful or large. Some were as big as houses. Others were as small as chickens. Some were meat eaters. Others, like Stegosaurus, were gentle plant eaters.

Cenozoic
(The era of mammals, including humans)

mammoth   *human*

Tertiary   **Quaternary**
65 million to   1.6 million
5 million   years ago
years ago   to today

Talk About Stegosaurus

Stegosaurus had bony plates
on its back.

The name *Stegosaurus* means "roof lizard." If Stegosaurus's rounded body were a house, its humped back would be the roof. And the strange, fanlike plates on its back would be the shingles.

Stegosaurus belonged to a group of dinosaurs called stegosaurs. They all had huge round bodies, tiny heads, and back legs that were longer than their front legs. Stegosaurus was the biggest and best known of the group.

Stegosaurus lived nearly 140 million years ago, in a time called the Jurassic period. It made its home in what is now North America. Long ago North America was different from the way it is today. A huge inland sea probably stretched down the middle, from Canada to the Gulf of Mexico. Many plants grew in the swampy land around the sea. Most likely that is where Stegosaurus lived.

Stegosaurus was huge. But its head was tiny— almost as small as a watermelon. And its brain was even smaller— no bigger than a golf ball.

 10

Stegosaurus had a very small head.
This is a side view of the creature's head.

11

Stegosaurus probably spent most of its day eating. Its tiny head was low to the ground. This made grazing on low plants like ferns easy. It snipped them off with its horny beak. Then it probably swallowed them whole.

Stegosaurus could probably stand on its rear legs in order to find other food.

Stegosaurus could probably also use its rear legs to stand up to reach higher leaves.

Stegosaurus was very strong, but probably very slow. It walked on all fours. It had big, flat feet like an elephant, with five hoofed toes on its front feet and three toes on its back feet. Because its back legs were much longer than its front legs, scientists think that Stegosaurus did not run. If it did, its back legs could have made it tumble over.

Stegosaurus may have used its tail to fight off other dinosaurs, such as Allosaurus.

Stegosaurus could not run from enemies. But it did have a weapon. Four to eight spikes— about 4 feet (1.2 m) long—grew out of its long, strong tail. Eyes on the side of its head let Stegosaurus see all around it. If a meat eater like Allosaurus came near, it could turn and use its tail like a big, spiky whip.

Stegosaurus laid large, oval eggs in nests.

 16

Scientists also think Stegosaurus traveled in herds. This probably helped it stay safe from attackers. And it likely helped it protect its young, too. No one is sure how Stegosaurus cared for its young. But adult and baby skeletons have been found together.

Like all dinosaurs, Stegosaurus laid eggs. Its eggs were large and oval. A baby Stegosaurus was about as big as a big dog. It had a horny beak. But it was not hatched with plates. These grew later.

As you can see, scientists have learned much about Stegosaurus. But there are still many mysteries to solve.

Unsolved Mysteries

The biggest question scientists have is what were Stegosaurus's back plates for? Experts once believed the plates were "armor" for protection, like the spikes on its tail. But now scientists think that the plates were probably too soft. Instead, most experts think they helped keep Stegosaurus cool in the summer and warm in the winter.

Stegosaurus's plates could keep the creature cool on hot days and warm on cold days.

18

Stegosaurus's plates ran from its neck to its tail. They contained blood vessels and were covered with skin. On a hot day a breeze blowing through them could cool Stegosaurus's blood. On a cold day the sun shining on them could warm Stegosaurus the same way.

Scientists also are not sure how these plates looked. Did they stick straight up? Or did they lie down? Were they lined up in one row or two?

And why were Stegosaurus's back legs so much longer than its front legs? Was it so Stegosaurus could stand on them and reach plants up above?

There is another mystery, too. How could such a huge creature have such a tiny brain? Some scientists think Stegosaurus must have had a second brain near its hip. They think that brain worked the dinosaur's tail and back legs. But other scientists say that whatever was there was not a brain. It is one of the mysteries that may be answered one day.

◀ Stegosaurus's plates may have stood straight up.

A model showing Stegosaurus's plates ▼

Stegosaurus
Stegosaurus had a narrow body and a heavy, spiked
back legs were almost twice as long as its front legs.
planteater may have reared on its hind legs to reach tall
vegetation.
Stegosaurus armatus

A Stegosaurus skeleton

Digging Up Answers

If you tried to find a Stegosaurus today, you could not. Stegosaurs—and all dinosaurs—no longer exist. Dinosaurs became extinct about 65 million years ago. So how do we know what we do about these reptiles from long ago? Scientists called paleontologists hunt for clues, mostly from fossils.

Fossils are remains of life long ago. They can be bones, footprints, or marks left in rocks. Fossils can show how big or how small a dinosaur was. They can show what it ate and how it moved.

Experts think that dinosaurs are extinct today because of a meteorite that hit Earth.

Fossils can tell us many things about how a dinosaur looked and lived. But there is one thing fossils have not shown us yet—why the dinosaurs disappeared.

 24

Most paleontologists believe that a giant rock from space, called a meteorite, hit Earth. When it hit, fires and tidal waves may have destroyed the places where dinosaurs lived. Other scientists think that a dust cloud blocked out the sunlight. Without sunlight, most plants would have died. Plant eaters like Stegosaurus would have had nothing to eat. And when all the plant eaters starved, meat eaters would have starved, too.

Other scientists think that Earth and its weather changed. The dinosaurs could not adapt to the new climates. Still others think a disease could have killed the creatures. Or maybe early mammals ate too many of the dinosaurs' eggs.

Although this odd "roof lizard" is gone, paleontologists keep digging for answers. Perhaps one day they will uncover all the mysteries of Stegosaurus.

Digging For Fossils

Finding fossils is fun and exciting. But it is also hard work. Paleontologists are people who study fossils. They really "rough it." The weather can be boiling hot or freezing cold. Strong winds can blow a whole camp away.

Every day on a dig seems long. Fossil hunters crawl on the ground, searching for good places to dig. Then they get to work with shovels, picks, brushes, and other tools.

Sometimes paleontologists spend many days sifting through dirt. Sometimes they spend a whole day searching and find nothing. Other times they discover large bones. Scientists harden the bones with a special glue. Then

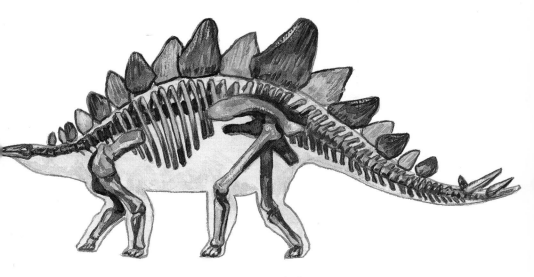

A Stegosaurus skeleton

the bones are carefully wrapped in heavy cloth and plaster of Paris. When the cast dries, the fossils are ready to be taken back to a museum.

Paleontologists carefully break the cast and cut it open. Then they gently blow or brush away the sand and dirt from the bones. They clean the bones. Then they glue any broken pieces into place. Whole dinosaur skeletons are rare. Sometimes paleontologists find bits and pieces of different skeletons. When they have enough parts, they are ready to put a whole dinosaur skeleton together!

Imprints in Time

Fossils can be very delicate. Paleontologists need to cover a fossil with a cast made of plaster of Paris. It is almost like a cast for a broken arm or leg.

Sometimes paleontologists do not find a bone. They may find a dinosaur footprint. Or they may find a skeleton print in a rock. When this happens, they fill the print with plaster. After the plaster dries, they have a perfect cast of the fossil print.

You can make a cast, too—even without a dinosaur fossil.

A cast of a Stegosaurus plate

 28

1. Take a jug of water, some plaster of Paris, and a bowl and a spoon for mixing.

2. Then search the woods or a field, even your backyard, for prints. Look for animal or human footprints, or leaf or plant prints in the mud. Or take a chicken bone and press it into a piece of clay.

3. Once you find a print, mix 2 parts plaster of Paris with 1 part water until smooth.

4. Then quickly (before it starts to get hard) pour the mixture into the print. Wait for the plaster to dry. (It may take up to half an hour.) Then lift the cast out of the print.

You will have a perfect fossil cast of prints from a deer hoof, cat paw, or sneaker bottom— the fossils of the future!

Glossary

adapt (uh-DAPT) Change in order to fit in and survive

Allosaurus (al-o-SORE-us) A huge meat-eating dinosaur that lived in North America during the Jurassic period

cast (KAST) A print made from an object, such as a fossil; a protective covering around an easily broken object, such as a fossil

dig (DIG) The event of digging in the earth for fossils or other dinosaur remains

dinosaurs (DIE-nuh-sores) Land-dwelling reptiles that lived from 245 million to 65 million years ago

extinct (ex-TINKT) No longer existing or living

fossil (FAH-sill) Remains of ancient life, such as a dinosaur bone, footprint, or imprint in a rock

Jurassic period (ju-RAS-ik) The time period from 208 million to 145 million years ago

 30

meteorite (MEE-tee-uh-rite) A rocky object from space that strikes the earth's surface; it can be a few inches or several miles wide

paleontologist (pay-lee-on-TAH-luh-jist) A scientist who studies fossils

reptile (REP-tile) A group of air-breathing animals that lay eggs and usually have scaly skin

stegosaur (STEG-uh-sore) A group of dinosaurs to which Stegosaurus belonged

Stegosaurus (steg-uh-SORE-us) A large plant-eating dinosaur that lived in North America during the Jurassic period

There were spikes on Stegosaurus's tail.

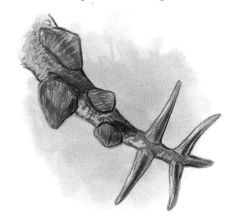

Index